A Craniosacral Story

by

Mary Nochimson, DC, LMT

ILLUSTRATED BY ISHIKA SHARMA

This book was created to help children understand the process of a particular medical treatment done by a trained professional. It is not intended as an instruction manual for this or any other treatments. The procedures depicted in the images and story should not be attempted by anyone other than a specially trained medical professional. Results of such treatments will vary.

A Crainiosacral Story

Copyright © 2020 Mary Nochimson, DC, LMT. All rights reserved, including the right to reproduce this book, or portions thereof, in any form. No part of this text may be reproduced, transmitted, downloaded, decompiled, reverse engineered, or stored in or introduced into any information storage and retrieval system, in any form or by any means, whether electronic or mechanical without the express written permission of the author. The scanning, uploading, and distribution of this book via the Internet or via any other means without the permission of the publisher is illegal and punishable by law. Please purchase only authorized editions and do not participate in or encourage electronic piracy of copyrighted materials.

The publisher does not have any control over and does not assume any responsibility for author or third-party websites or their content.

Illustrated by Ishika Sharma

Published by Telemachus Press, LLC
7652 Sawmill Road, Suite 304
Dublin, Ohio 43016
http://www.telemachuspress.com

Follow the author on Instagram:
@ better.every.step.today

ISBN: 978-1-951744-46-5 (Paperback)

Version 2020.11.16

This book is dedicated to

Dr. John Upledger

The Pioneer in Craniosacral Therapy

A Craniosacral Story

Hi my name is John and this is my Craniosacral story.

Craniosacral is a special place for me
where I can discover truths about my body,
and Mary joins me on my journey.

Mary does not make my body do
things it does not want to do.

She understands I am perfect the way I am
no matter what I decide to do.

Whenever I go, I lie on a massage table
which looks like a bed
where Mary places her hands on my head.

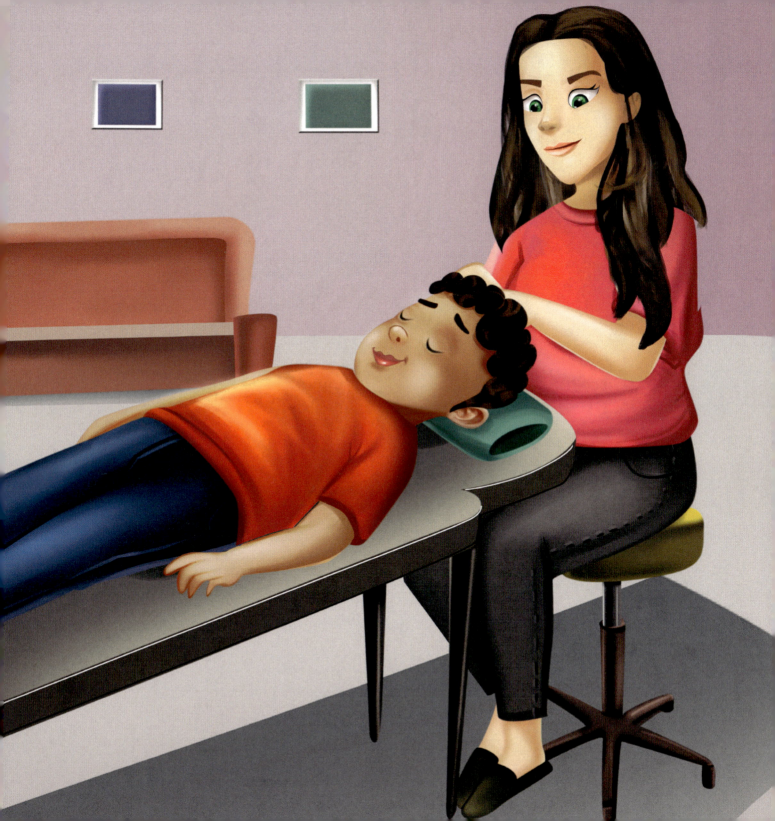

I close my eyes and go into a trance,
and now my body begins the dance.

Mary places her hands on my tummy and back
and now I feel very relaxed.

The tummy rumbling is being heard.
That must be due to the vagus nerve.

She rocks my dural tube to and fro.
It reminds me of when I was with mommy in-utero.

She pulls on one ear and then pulls on two.
It feels like she is releasing the head glue!

My brain takes a great big "sigh."
My brain is happier and now so am I!

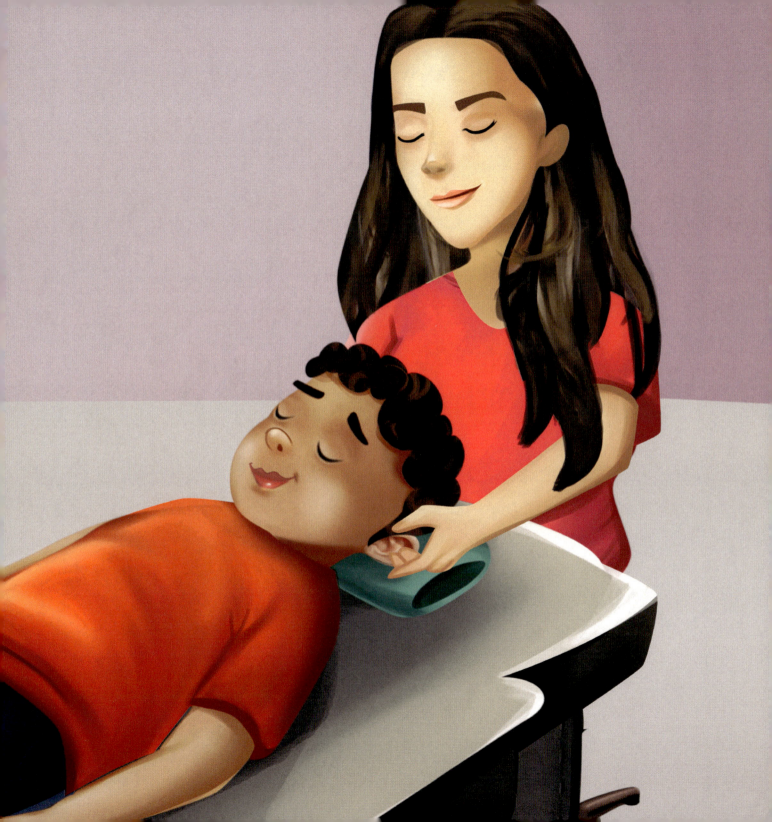

Sometimes she rubs my teeth & my gums along with my cheeks, palate and tongue.

Before I was stressed to be alive.
But not anymore
since the release of cranial nerve five.

I remembered when I was just one,
I do not remember it being so fun.

I could not eat and did not know why.
On the massage table, I started to cry.
Was it the plagio, torticollis,
an allergy or a lip or tongue tie?

I just remember the struggle was real,
but it was not the time or day.
So, I packaged it in an energy cyst
and stored it away.

It was time to let that go now,
so I told Mary the what, where, when, why and how.

All of a sudden my body began to squirm,
getting rid of this memory like I was fighting a germ.

Next my body started to wiggle and jiggle,
and then I started to giggle.

The painful memory has gone away,
never to be in my body another day.

Giggles HaHa Giggles
HaHa HaHa

The session has come to an end.

I gave Mary a hug and said,
"Thanks, I feel so brand new!"
She said,
"Do not thank me. It was all your Inner Doc and You!"

I asked, "May I ask my Inner Doc questions, would that be okay?"

She said, "Absolutely, yes! That is always alright any time, night or day."

Now when you go to your Craniosacral Therapist, you won't have to worry!

About the Author

Mary Nochimson, DC, LMT "Dr. Mary," is a Broward County Chiropractor devoted to improving lives through a variety of modalities. In addition to being a licensed Doctor of Chiropractic, she's also a certified acupuncturist and licensed massage therapist. Her other certifications include ashiatsu, bamboosage, Craniosacral Therapy (CS1, CS2, Peds 1, Peds 2) and NAET (Nambudripad's Allergy Elimination Technique). When patients seek health options other than, or in addition to, medications and surgery, Dr. Mary has much to offer. She can combine these therapies for best results, and frequently employs several into one treatment session.

She is clearly not your mother's chiropractor with such a variety of therapies at her fingertips, but for those who appreciate the conventional medical model, it should be noted she has worked alongside respected medical doctors at an internal medicine practice in the Sunrise/Lauderhill area for thirty years. When patients with headaches, neck pain, joint, muscle or low back pain visit, they have a choice of traditional medicine and/or alternative healthcare.

You can follow Dr. Mary on Instagram at:

@ better.every.step.today

Made in the USA
Columbia, SC
27 August 2022